Joy in a Box

and other stories

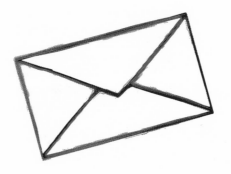

SALLY HANAN

Joy in a Box
By Sally Hanan
Copyright 2009, 2014 Sally Hanan

"The Spider and the Fly" is a poem by Mary Howitt (1799–1888), published in 1829. This work is in the public domain worldwide.

Cover & interior design: Allison Metcalfe Design
Editing team: Inksnatcher and Strong Tower Publishing

ISBN: 978-0-9913350-3-9
Publisher: Fire Drinkers Publishing

To Gerry, Becky, and Zack.
Without you, my life would not be so full of joy.

Table of Contents

Table Of Contents

Joy In A Box

1

Joy In A Box

I stepped inside as he was hanging the last painting. It was, somehow, a comforting place to be, in spite of the white walls and well-hung portraits. In a way, the austerity added to the warmth. I lingered by the first picture. It was of a little boy playing in the sand. His face captured my attention, making my eyes wait for longer than was comfortable. Looking straight at me was joy personified.

I couldn't move on, and the gallery owner shuffled and wheezed to my side.

"That's Kurt." He rubbed a tired finger under his round nose. I like to remember them in their best moment. He was shot down in the summer of '65; died in a lot of pain."

I glared at the floor as I stepped away. I liked to make my own observations.

The next one was a beauty! She sat sideways on a kitchen chair, hand on her growing belly, her smile causing her whole face to come alive. As I leaned in, I could see her smile directed toward a man, probably her husband.

"That was the last time she smiled like that. I lost her in childbirth."

I shuddered. Here on the walls was no misery, only happiness. Why did he have to spoil my enjoyment?

I frowned at him, moving fast across the room to another framed capture. This woman had dusty gray hair, with the wrinkles of time tucked into her contented face. There was such depth to her, such a sense of fullness....

"That's Victoria."

I could hear him inhaling, ready for the next sentence, but I turned to face him. "I'm sorry, sir, but I came in here to look, not listen, and you're making it very difficult for me to do that."

His saddened eyes surveyed the floor. Finally, they moved back up to my face.

"Lady? I'm Jack, and this is my family. These here people are all I've got left. Each one was in my heart and in my life; now they're all in Someone else's arms. I painted these here walls white to help remind me of where they went, but I painted their faces to remind me of who they were.

"See Kurt here? I watched him die. Was holding his hand as he opened those eyes of his for a second, and then I saw him smile his last time. It reminded me of the time we was on the beach as kids, me 'n my brother. I wanted to remember that time, not the time he left me.

"That old lady there? She's my mom. Great lady that one. Never a cross word in the house with her around. She'd take my daddy aside and say, 'Now John, them kids gotta stay kids. Time enough to change their ways when 'n if they get old enough to bother other people.'

"And this beauty? Well, she's special. She loved me like no woman has ever loved a man." He sighed a deep sigh and gently touched the outline of her lips. As he did so, his smile began to return.

Now I understood. I took his warm hand and placed it in my palm. He seemed puzzled, but smiled back anyhow. I wanted to explain to him what he had just done, but I couldn't put it into words.

"I'll be back; I promise."

A month later, I took the tram back to the little gallery. Under my arm was a scrapbook—nothing much to look at from the outside, but deep within its pages were some mementos of my own. I practically ran to the door of the place. When I got there, all I saw through the window was a collection of questionable plastic forms and a glittery red vulture at the door.

"Where's the old man, Jack, the painter who was here last month?"

"Oh, DARLing, he died. DO come inside and have some cocktails. I'd LOVE to show you my Venus."

I pulled away from her talons and started to walk the other way.

"DO come again, DARLing. We have a special on the Eros figurine. It was imported from IIIIItaly."

Within minutes, the tears were dripping off my chin and onto my scarf. On examination, I could see that my mascara obviously wasn't as waterproof as the ads had claimed it to be. To my right were the steps to a townhouse, which I took as an invitation and sat down. The scrapbook pages I had longed to open to Jack now opened to me, each smile and grin and beam reaching out to embrace me. I started to smile with them; in fact, I even began to laugh.

Jack had given me this gift. He didn't need reminders of his joy anymore. He was living it. And because of him, I now had some joy of my own, all encased in a little unassuming scrapbook. One day, I would get to meet my mom and my dear sweet David again. Until then, I had their smiles, and they weren't boxed up on the top shelf of my closet, along with my joy, anymore.

~

A Gift...
A Friend...
A Foe

~

2
A Gift…A Friend…A Foe

She played with her fingers outside the courtroom. The lines on her palms were deeper these days. Blue veins thudded their contents across the back of her hand. A white smudge under the nail of her left index finger captured her scrutiny. *A gift, a friend, a foe . . .* Frank had taught her that old childhood rhyme back in third grade. He'd always been the superstitious one. What would he say now, now that her index nail was telling her that another enemy was on its way?

The bench was hard . . . cold. Lawyers stood around in their pressed suits, fingers curled around briefcase handles. A man around the corner spoke of his wife's adultery loud enough for all and sundry to hear. It was a nasty business—divorce. That was not why Ella sat there, though. Frank was dead. The kids wanted his money.

Frank had been good to her. He had been good to his children too; his kids, not hers. Golf club memberships, homes in the hills, nice cars, speeding tickets, bail bonds—nothing was too much for Frank's wallet. He loved them. They wanted the love to continue, and they knew that Ella was a fan of tough love. They had fired up their pumiced hides in opposition.

Ella rubbed a black mark on the floor with her shoe tip. She liked things to be clean. This was a messy business.

It had been a sad few months. Frank was lowered into

the ground on a sunny day in March. The clocks sprang forward, and so did the children—on their cell phones to their lawyers. What they had feared most had come true: Frank had left Ella his entire fortune.

False love turned into guilt that turned into manipulation that turned into threats. They videotaped her. They followed her. They bugged her home. And now it was June; now it was time.

The attorney pushed his head out the door and jerked it. Ella stood up. She picked some lint off her skirt. She walked into the courtroom. Smug faces abounded from every pew. Ella held onto the desk as she eased herself into the defendant's chair.

Their lawyer was good. She was shrewd and sharp. She moved from accusations of mental trauma to disabilities to emotional stress—all Ella's fault. Ella really didn't look like a stable person by the time the lawyer was through. And then came Ella's turn.

Ella patted her coiffed head. Frank had always said that she should be on stage. Today was her day. She laughed, she cried, she cajoled, she reminisced. Her slideshow captured the laziness and lies of every family member over the previous decade. By the end of her expository, Ella had brought the crowd (all but the sullen children) to its feet. The months of drama and speech classes had paid off. The last thing anyone in the room could have pinned on her was the craziness Frank's descendants were accusing her of. She sat down, panting somewhat with the exertion of it all, but with the right corner of her mouth tucked up into a checkered smile of victory.

The judge shook his head in awe as he removed his little round glasses to run a finger and thumb down his eyebrows. Once Ella was comfortably seated again, he leaned into the microphone and glared at the prosecutors.

"I suggest you learn what the word JOB means, as you will have to have one for the rest of your lives." He brought down the gavel with a thud. "Case dismissed."

The last few stragglers left the room, leaving only Ella and a security guard. She chose to go out the back door. There was no point in leaving any loose ends.

She lifted her legs onto the leather seats of Frank's awaiting limousine. Frank's hand reached out for hers and lifted her fingers to his lips. He noticed the white spot on her index nail and laughed.

"I guess you made some enemies today."

Ella chuckled. "All in a day's work . . . something those leeches will learn soon enough."

"So it worked? We're really free from giving them handouts for the rest of our lives?"

Ella grinned and nodded. "It's all ours now, Frank. I couldn't have done it without you." She rested her head on his shoulder.

He sighed in satisfaction.

She stroked the revolver in her purse. He was the enemy now. As soon as the bank accounts were unfrozen, Frank would truly be . . . a dead man.

The Gin
Stockpile

3

The Gin Stockpile

Momma's got the shakes tonight. She got drunk. She said she weren't drunk on nothin' but the Holy Spirit, but I know better. I seen her sneak out, sneaked out she did, right after dinner. She said she were goin' to the store, but I seen her; I seen her go to the Chapel of the Holy Ghost. I think they be drinkin' in there. They must be to have Marla's momma be so far gone now.

Now she be sittin' across from me at the table, gigglin' and shakin' and acting all stupid. I don't know where she gone got the money from. Maybe she has some old boy down at the chapel givin' her gin for some lovin' from her bony frame. Dirty old man! Wait 'til I get my hands on him. I asked Marla where her momma be gettin' all the shakes from. She says it be from the chapel. I never seen anyone shakin' from chapel. Marla says there be a revival goin' on down there these nights, and that I should go; it might go and do me some good.

Good, huh? Like I could get it any better than this? I got Momma cookin' my dinner and Marla in my bed, and between them they look after the little brats—all five of them. I ain't got nothin' to complain about.

But this has me thinkin'. What if she got some gin party goin' on? I could get me some from that dirty old man and then beat him up good after I find his stock.

I followed Momma tonight. Now I know why she gets

those shakes, or . . . I think I do. That old lady sorta ran down to the chapel. The room was packed. They had some sort of visiting preacher woman. Her name was Katherine somethin' or other; I don't remember now; but it was like she had a halo around her, sort of light and floatin'. There was people in wheelchairs there. I stood in the dark in the back row, but that lady did point her bony finger into the darkness and call me right out, yes she did. She said I had a problem with my heart. How did she know my heart skipped and danced like a striped bumble bee? I felt a tinglin' and then a heat crawl through my chest and then it stopped. Momma slapped her hands onto her mouth when she saw me, and then she smiled. I don't know why she gone smiled like that.

That's when that lady, she asked me if I knew Jesus.

I said, "Well no, Ma'am, I can't say I do."

She stared me down, and then she told me that it was Jesus who gone and fixed my heart, and that he could fix my life too.

Like I said, I had it good, and I was about to tell her that too when I got to cryin' like a big baby. Somethin' got a hold of me and wouldn't let go. She told me that was Jesus, and that he would let me go if I told him I was sorry for my sin. Sin? That's when I felt real bad and wanted to feel clean like the light around that lady. I didn't know what to do, but she told me to copy what she said, so I said, "I'm sorry for my sin, Jesus. I'll do whatever you want from here on out."

That's when it happened. I started to feel washed out, like nothin' heavy was left there anymore. Momma walked up to me in her crooked way and put her hand on my shoulder. She was shakin', and then I got to shakin'. We shook our way home, laughin' together like two coyotes.

Marla thinks I'm fakin' it, but Momma says that time will tell. I wouldn't fake somethin' that looks so stupid.

So much for that gin stockpile. Now I guess I got me some Jesus.

A Fat Lot
of Use

4
A Fat Lot of Use

It was a Monday when it began.

"Vines," my editor said, "go with a vines theme. We're putting a book together: an anthology of short stories, prose, and poetry, and we'd like your writing in it. Unfortunately, your deadline is Sunday night. Can you get it in by then?" I could hear her apologetic, yet hopeful, tone.

"Sure, no problem."

A sigh of relief came from the other end of the phone.

Flattered by her enthusiasm for my work, my cinematographic mind whirred into action.

On Monday, I visualized a woman's bejeweled hand slowly disappearing under a buffed rug of murdering tendrils. Despite the killer ending, the story line remained elusive.

On Tuesday, I saw a young man rejected by love's first kiss, and he entered the vine-covered monastery walls to dedicate his life to prayer and artistic pursuits. His choice caused many sinners to be brought to salvation through his painstakingly copied holy books and his long hours of intercession on a chilled stone floor.

Wednesday showed me Rapunzel climbing out the narrow tower window and down the wall of vines, alone, after strangling the evil witch with her shorn braids.

(Prince Charming didn't respond fast enough.)

Thursday's vine was a big, leafy, fruity bush with one wide bare branch that hung out near the ground. It fed off and passed on gossip (hence the song, "Heard It on the Grapevine"), until God came along with his big pruning shears and lopped it off. Just because it was an impressively big and obvious branch didn't make it necessary.

Friday had me thinking about the kudzu vine, which has taken over an estimated seven million acres of the US Southeast countryside. It is not considered a helpful plant at all, like some people I have had the pleasure of working with.

On Saturday, I thought of how vines can become the staple support system of the walls they grow on, and how, if the owner tries to remove them, the walls collapse. Certain individuals think their churches would crumble without them. Fortunately, many others are like those supportive vines, growing together and strengthening each other to build God's kingdom.

Now it is Sunday. I'm thinking of a "young knockout marries old geezer with loads of money" type of story. Her main focus is looking good to others, so she whips the gardens at the mansion into shape for future outdoor parties. Her evil stepchildren (who really want all their dad's money for themselves) plant a single vine in a shady corner, where she won't see it. It begins to take over every flowerbed until it starts to cover her—a mix of Monday and Friday's ideas.

The thing is, it is still Sunday, and I have yet to send any completed inspiration on to my editor. I have, however, learned an incredibly important life lesson. Writers can have the greatest ideas in the world, but they are a fat lot of use to anyone if they don't take the time to fulfill the assignments given them.

PS My editor is looking for new writers . . . for an assignment due in tonight . . . any takers?

PPS Don't tell her I referred you.

Out of the
Darkness

5
Out of the Darkness

We called him Mr. Bobby. I thought he was just like all the other white people who had come to our home in Mozambique—someone who loved Jesus—but when I saw what happened that night, I knew that he doesn't just love Jesus; he walks with God.

That night, Momma Heidi wanted to go to one of the villages, where a team was going to show the *JESUS** movie, and she asked Mr. Bobby to go with her. I begged and begged her to let me go, because she likes me to translate for her sometimes when the words are difficult, and she said yes!

We drove for a long time, and I could see the lights flickering near the huts as the Jeep pulled nearer. Momma Heidi jumped out; she's always excited about people seeing the movie and hearing about Jesus. I am too. I ran with her. I looked back while I was running after Momma, and Mr. Bobby was getting out of the Jeep slowly. He looked tired, so I ran back to him and took his hand. He rubbed my hair and smiled at me. I like Mr. Bobby's smiles.

Just when we were getting near the sitting people, Mr. Bobby stopped.

"Run over there," he whispered, like there was danger, so I ran to one of the huts and lay down. Mr. Bobby turned to look in the other direction, and out of the darkness I saw them: three men, and they looked very bad. The first man was a voodoo man. His face was all white and was painted with some black marks. I've never seen a face before like his. It made me want to scream and get sick and run away, all at the same time. The second man was one of the men we have seen before. He makes a lot of trouble for Momma and Poppa. He says Allah is God, but he is not. All the time, he tries to get men angry and throw stones and burn down houses. He had a big stick in his hands. The third man had a bottle in his hands, and he looked like he was going to fall over.

Then I started to see many men behind them, all holding things to hurt people with.

I looked at Momma Heidi with the village people. She had not seen the bad men. We needed help, and we needed it fast. Momma Heidi could not stop these men, but my God could. I began to pray, but I kept my eyes open.

Mr. Bobby curled his finger at the priest.

"Come here," he said.

My mouth must have been open because the back of my throat went all dry. Did he not know how powerful the priests were? The priest's eyes would have burned me into a heap of ashes if he had looked at me the way he looked at Mr. Bobby. The priest stayed where he was.

"In the name of Jesus, I command you to come here."

My chin must have hit the ground when I saw the priest run and stop a little bit away from Mr. Bobby. Then I saw Mr. Bobby lift up his hand. I heard a big noise like thunder, and from Mr. Bobby's hand came a rope of lightening. The lightening hit the priest, and his body was flung up really high into the air, and then it was thrown over the village huts and we all heard it thump onto the ground.

The bad men's white bits around their eyes got bigger and bigger, and then they all sort of screamed at the same time, and they ran really, really fast, far away.

Mr. Bobby's chest went out in a big heave and so did mine. He stood there for a few minutes in silence. I said nothing. I was still shaking. Then he turned around and smiled at me.

"Rashid," he said, "we have a very big God, and he cares about this village." Then he walked to me, took my hand, and we went to tell Momma Heidi about how we almost died.

This is based on a true story Bobby Connors told about his trip to Mozambique in 2005. Everything he did in those moments was in obedience to what God told him to do. Afterwards, he heard that every deaf person in the village was miraculously healed the moment the voodoo priest landed on the ground.

Read about Heidi and Rolland Baker's ministry in Mozambique:
   » *http://www.irismin.org/p/background.php*
   » *http://www.jesusfilm.org/*

~

Roses Are Red

~

6
Roses Are Red

Walter's bulbous fingertips prodded out each letter with care.

Roses are red,

Violets are blue...

Walter grimaced at how uncreative he was, and, to add to his frustration, the computer was still not acting like a trusted friend. Marie, his first true love—always patient, always kind—would have helped him. Now she was with the Lord, and he'd have to struggle through it alone. He hushed the grief that stirred in his stomach.

The bouquet of pink and white flowers, which had just set him back a pretty penny, lay beside the monitor. Walter had never bought Louise flowers before, but he wanted this visit to be different: something Louise didn't expect, something that would make her feel special, and today was Valentine's Day. He had wanted to pick her flowers from his garden, but truth to tell, his green fingers had fallen to his sides after Marie's death.

Shaking hands reached out to the keyboard again. The raised veins trembled in anticipation, but the fingers never hit the raised squares. They stood, immobilized in the fear of doing it wrong.

Walter pushed back from the monitor for a moment, shaking his head in dismay. This wasn't going to be quite as easy as he'd thought. He reached in and scratched his hairy ear. *Got to speed up. My second true love is waiting on me.*

She was waiting on him, sort of. This was her shift at the diner, and he always came in at the same time: 4 p.m. It was the quietest time of her working day, and Louise would usually sit with him and listen to his stories.

Walter bowed his head and prayed for inspiration. As he lifted his humble head, a warm glow of a smile stretched across his face, stretching the gnarls of years gone by. Like percolating coffee, the flow from his brain filtered through his fingers.

It's the way you care, Louise.

When I speak, you listen to each word. I love the way your hair settles gently on your face, and that little curl that rests on your shoulder that you flick off impatiently.

I love the way you sit at the table with me and make me feel like I am your only customer.

I love that you won't let me tip you, saying that I'm family and you wouldn't dare.

I love to watch you at work. You're so efficient, so quick to take care of everyone.

You remind me of my first love. I know, I know, I shouldn't be talking about another woman on Valentine's Day of all days, but I recognize the characteristics of a great woman when I see them, and you have them, just like she did. I miss her, but I know you understand. That's just the way you are, my perfect girl.

Walter leaned back in the library chair in satisfaction. *Thank you for understanding too, Lord, and thanks for the help with this contraption.* As he patted the monitor, the printer jumped into life. After a few whirrs, the finished love letter was in a pink envelope and gently centered within the roses. His arthritic hand held the base of the bouquet tightly as he crossed Main Street, the noise of traffic dull in his ears.

Sneaking in while she wasn't looking, he stood by the door for a few minutes to watch her and to savor the thrill of being able to love so much. The mix of pale colors, scent, and petals were set softly on the slippery diner seat.

He caught her eye. Grinning as he beckoned her over to his table, he pulled out the flowers. She shook her head, in shock but smiling. He was almost breathing on her in his eagerness to see her reaction to his card. Pulling the envelope out of the seductive scent, her eyes questioned his. He nodded encouragingly.

Everyone who worked in the diner loved Louise, and their happiness for her as she smiled through her tears hovered tenderly in the silence. Walter held up a napkin and gently dabbed her eyes.

"How about a big hug for an old man on a special day, sweetheart?" His arms opened wide and Louise fell into them.

Louise's father's arms had always been a place of comfort and love, and now, on St. Valentine's Day, she couldn't think of any place she'd rather be.

Blogspot 90210

7
Blogspot 90210

This is a parody on the misplaced zeal of brand-new believers. If you have been on the receiving end of such fervor, I apologize on behalf of all Christians.

When I read about the All Nations College Campout, I was SO excited! Now that I've finished my evangelism course, I can't wait to try out all of the techniques I've learned on all the idolaters and sinners I'll find there. I leave on Friday after lunch, and it's over after a peace service on Sunday.

Blogspot 90211

Back at last! It was such an awesome time! The first thing I did when I got there was to find the best spot to set up my tent—you know, near the faucet and the restrooms. I found one, but someone else wanted it too. She looked like she was from India, so I stood my ground. After all, I knew God would want me to have the best place so that I was blessed as his child. After I set up my tent, I chased her down and asked her all about her beliefs. She was setting up her tent in an okay spot, so I talked while she worked. Turns out she was Hindu, so I'm sure I impressed her with everything I'd learned about Hinduism. I got her on every argument she had; now I'm going to pray for her to see the light and really think about how wrong she is. I can't remember her name now; I hope that doesn't matter when I'm praying.

The bell rang for dinner that night, and I made sure I was one of the first in line. I threw on an extra chunk of cheese when the server wasn't looking, because I'd forgotten to make sure I had my five ounces of dairy that morning. It's very important to be obedient to the Lord in everything, and that includes making sure my body gets what it needs. While I was eating, I noticed that some of the people at the end didn't have enough food. I guess they should have been faster at getting in line.

The next morning I sat under the most central tree and opened up my biggest Bible. It was a bit awkward, making sure that everyone could see the outside cover, which said HOLY BIBLE, but I managed it. Anything for the Lord. I also turned up my CD player to "superloud" and played "Our God Is an Awesome God" over and over. I needed to make sure that everyone knew what I stood for.

Once the professor had finished his talk on campus communication that afternoon, I made sure to ask loud questions about religious groups and their methods of communiqué. People need to know that we Christians are not a minority and need to be consulted before anything is organized. After all, we are a majority in the government.

Later that day I went around and passed out the tracts I'd made about hell. They had such awesome drawings! I'd spent ages making sure the flames were the right shade of orange and red, and I'm so thankful to the Lord for giving me the gift. I'd entitled them TURN OR BURN. It seemed apt when I was in the midst of such a cesspool of iniquity.

It *poured* rain that night, and one couple had the nerve to ask me if they could share my tent. They'd been camping in the woods and all their stuff was wet. I figured it was the time to give them a lecture on the consequences of their sin of sleeping together before marriage and told them that God was judging them with the rain for their choices. I told them I'd let them in if they repented and chose Jesus as their lord and savior, but they told me I could . . . well, it's too embarrassing to rewrite here. I've been praying for them—that they would learn to choose righteousness over their sinful, lustful, fleshly desires.

I could not believe the peace service on Sunday! The teacher had the nerve to say that we all had the same God and went on and on about how we were one world and could be one people group. It was all so shocking! I muttered many things, and I made sure I was loud enough for those around me to hear so that they could be sure to choose the right path.

Overall, I am very excited about how far I got with my evangelism. This is definitely my gifting, and I hope to do more very soon. Come Lord Jesus!

The author must alert you to the fact that she has had absolutely no personal immersion in the behavior or thoughts of the aforementioned teenager.

A Distant Presence

8

A Distant Presence

He lifted one foot up from the wrinkled rock beneath him and moved it forward to its next new territory to claim. The ocean lay before him, immeasurable and mesmerizing.

Only water met his sole, down . . . down . . . down . . . until his whole body tilted and yanked his head after it. The quick breath he had taken before going under was shallow, as shallow as the water above the bank of rock he had fallen from. Some deeper part of him roared, grasping for life and breath and solid ground. Arms, legs, hair—all flailed together—until it occurred to him to turn back to the step he had taken for granted, the one he had lifted his foot off, the one that had held him so explicitly and steadfastly only seconds before. It was the only security he had known.

He could not find it. He could only sense its distant presence.

Panic filled his gut.

The trust he had placed in the rock had been blind, yet the rock had let him fall, had let him move forward without grasping or calling him home. He began to see that his place on that stony bank had been held with his own acquiescence, with his arms and hands and willingness to move with the flow of the tide.

The unprocessed fear dissipated. He motioned his arms

up and down into a slower, rhythmic motion that sliced through the gentle waves pushing against his torso. His feet and legs flexed and pointed and kicked until his face rose through the watery ceiling above him. His mouth opened to imbibe the salty air in triumph.

The step was still there, close by, somewhere, but it had led him to the edge of the world ahead, and

now that he was in it,

he knew

he could swim.

In the Orange-Sherbet Light

9
In the Orange-Sherbet Light

Aunt Dot lifted her shaky hand to her bifocals, lowered
them to her nose, and squinted in my direction.

"Eh?"

I cupped my fingers around my mouth and shouted
again, "I *love* this book!"

She smiled—one of those fizzy drink kind of smiles that
pops tiny bubbles of air to the lips over seconds of time.
Then she went back to reading.

The fire's flames started to slumber. Tiny rippling snores
trickled through the warm air to my ears. Dot was asleep.
We'd been sitting in our lush armchairs for hours, and
my rear was starting to protest. I lifted the bookmark
from the arm of the chair and lodged it deep between
the pages, as per Aunt Dot's training.

Taking off my own reading glasses, I glanced over at
Dot. At eighty-five, she was a marvelous mystery to all
who met her, especially her doctor. She had survived
the death of two husbands and a child, and suffered
from some bone disease she couldn't pronounce. Maybe
knowing death so intimately was why she reached out to
me, maybe not. I'll never truly figure out why she did it.

She'd invited me over for a glass of lemonade after
Dad's funeral. I left Mom lying in her bed, her back
to the door. Dot greeted me with an all-encompassing
hug that managed to make me feel loved, understood,

and special all in one touch. "Call me Aunt Dot," she'd said. We sat in her living room, eating ginger snaps and drinking cocoa. Even then, there was no need for talk. She brought me a pile of old hardback books, sat them like a treasure chest onto the cushion beside me, and opened the top one. Her voice didn't crackle back then.

"'Mrs. Rachel Lynde lived just where the Avonlea main road dipped down into a little hollow, fringed with alders and ladies' eardrops and traversed by a brook that had its source away back in the woods of the old Cuthbert place. . . .'"

I was hooked.

We traveled through many places that year and all those since. Avonlea, Robinson Crusoe's island, Sunnybrook Farm, under the sea, all the way to China. We were somewhere in Europe when Mom died, and Dot gave me another one of those hugs and said that she wanted to adopt me, just as Rachel Lynde adopted Anne. I cried and gave her a shaky smile, and that was that.

I made it through high school, falling asleep most nights with a book on my chest and my mind elsewhere. I survived college. I did the whole marriage, kids, retirement thing.

So here I was, aged sixty-six, coming to the end of our monthly fireside get-together. I walked softly to Dot's sleeping side and lifted the glasses off her face. The orange sherbet light fluttered over her crinkled countenance, highlighting her laughter lines, accentuating her warmth. I bookmarked her page, set the tale on the floor, and leaned forward to kiss her forehead.

"Eh?" Her eyes opened.

I hopped backwards.

A grin burst onto her face. "Hello, sweetie. Did you say something?"

"Yes . . . no . . . um, well . . . you know, Dot . . ." I paused to find the perfect words but couldn't. "Just . . . thank you."

She kneaded her eyes with her bony knuckles. "For what, child?"

My own were beginning to fill up. "For everything."

Dot patted my hand. "Silly girl."

For some reason, that made me cry more. She heaved her body forward, stretched out her arms to her walker, and I helped her to her feet. She hoisted the frame in tiny lifts to face me. Her eyes used their laser power to capture mine, to make sure that not one word was missed.

"Sweetie, having you in my life has been the biggest blessing God could ever give a woman. Don't go thanking me. You've brought me joy." She leaned forward against the edge of her metal support and gave me one of those hugs.

I cried and gave her a shaky smile, and that was that.

Will You Walk Into My Parlor?

10

Will You Walk Into My Parlor?

She sits in there, in her white brick room beside the highway. The painted words on her outer wall call out to drivers like me. PSYCHIC READINGS. The letters curl at the ends like beckoning fingers, luring me in to see my future spread out on her lacy table.

"Will you walk into my parlor?" said the Spider to the Fly,

"'Tis the prettiest little parlor that ever you did spy;"

One building down from her is the collision center. Their advertising is less enticing: A '70s Oldsmobile has been purposefully crashed into a fake wall, and there is no sign of it ever recovering. Does she realize the irony of her location?

"The way into my parlor is up a winding stair,

And I have many curious things to show you when you are there."

I drive by her shack of divinity twice a week, on my way to church. I drive by tonight and push my usual *pshaw* of noisy judgmental air through my lips, when I hear: *PRAY for her.* That's all he says.

"Oh no, no," said the Fly, "to ask me is in vain;

For who goes up your winding stair can ne'er come down again."

I push back on the steering wheel in surprise. I check the outside of her devilish hut, sideways (just in case she sees me looking), to see if I'm missing something. *But God, wouldn't that . . . don't I have to LIKE someone before I pray for her? Besides, what if she telepathically hears me pray and sucks me into her netherworld of evil?*

"Oh no, no," said the little Fly, "for I've often heard it said

They never, never wake again, who sleep upon your bed!"

My mind heads for the runway and begins to speed up.

Scenario 1:

I sneak up on the place in the dark of night and walk around the walls of her psychic stronghold seven times. On the stroke of midnight, I whip out my gold (well, gold-colored) ram's horn, blow for all I'm worth, and the walls fall down. Voila! She has no den of iniquity to serve in.

The brain cells turn faster.

Scenario 2:

I curse the place, it disappears in a horrible fire, and all of her fiendish instruments collect in the puddled ashes. (The lace tablecloth should catch the flames particularly nicely.) Voila! She has no occultic base to spread her poison from.

"Oh no, no," said the little Fly, "kind sir, that cannot be,

I've heard what's in your pantry, and I do not wish to see!"

Smoke is coming out of my ears.

Scenario 3:

Yelling in tongues, I storm into the stronghold of Satan. I point my gold-leafed, six-hundred-page Bible toward her bosom and yell, "Be gone, ye spirits of darkness!"

Instantly, she slumps to the floor, while the smell of sulphur creeps out of the room on all fours. Voila! She opens one eye and murmurs,

"Wow, you are so awesome!"

"Sweet creature," said the Spider, "you're witty   and you're wise;

How handsome are your gauzy wings, how brilliant are your eyes!"

We have gray matter take-off.

Scenario 4:

I do what God's asked me to do, and I begin to pray.

I stop at the lights and check my teeth in the mirror. I think I'll go with number 3.

With buzzing wings she hung aloft, then near and nearer drew,

Thinking only of her brilliant eyes, and green and purple hue;

Pictures form. In my mind, I pull up beside her red Mazda that's parked by the front door. I lean my eyes into her back window with cupped hand to see a car seat belted in place. Fast food bags litter the floor.

I enter to find a foyer of sorts. Pink frills surround the solitary seat cushion, and a granddaughter's school drawing is pressed to the wall with a thumbtack. A hand appears through the beads, followed by a large maternal body.

"Hello, sweetie. You here to have your fortune read?" Her smile is one of heartache and struggle.

Unto an evil counselor close heart, and ear, and eye,

And take a lesson from this tale of the Spider and the Fly.

A word that's fitly spoken can cut through deepest bone,

Lord take me from your quiver, and shoot this arrow home.

I stop the car and breathe. The pictures fade.

God, I'm so sorry, and I begin to pray.

The Collection

11
The Collection

It was grubby. The work of a two-year-old. Yet something drew the man to its pigments and lines, like a child's hands to a lightening bug.

"Whatcha think, Jesse? Will we send old meanie Grandpa a card?"

"Yeah!" Jesse clapped her hands. Ryan smirked at her naiveté and rolled the crayons in her direction. He regretted it already, but maybe . . . Whatever.

Jesse's tubby hands sat on the waxen mass as she filled in what remained of the empty space on the card. She couldn't read the print.

MERRY CHRISTMAS, DAD

Ryan decided not to add anything to it. He'd already said enough.

His trembling fingers turned the card from right to left, the light casting a net of color on his pupils. It had been a year since he'd received the last one. He walked backwards until his shaky legs found a solid seat.

Water pumped into his cloudy eyes. He let a drop roll steadily down past his jawbone and onto the myriad of color. His Sheltie walked up to his side and leaned his head on his hand. A small corner of the man's mouth turned upward as his fingers curved through the warmth of his dog's hair.

"I'm gonna give him a biiiig kiss."

Ryan smiled halfheartedly at his daughter without really seeing her.

She picked up the card and planted a huge wet smacker over her artwork. Then she kissed all over the rest of the card. "So he can have lots of love," she explained. She stood up on Ryan's lap and stared into his eyes. "Just like you, Daddy. You give me lots of love," and she planted another sloppy wet one on his mouth.

He grunted and kissed her forehead. How could I not love you?

They walked to the mail box together. Her little feet were steadier these days, her curls beginning to straighten out. Both of his strong hands gripped her chubby waist and lifted her to the flap, which she pulled down eagerly.

"Now Grandpa will get his Kissmas card, won't he, Daddy, won't he, cuz I gave him a lots of kisses on it?"

"Yes, sweetie; he will."

Jesse's grandpa leaned forward to let the table take his weight as he rose. He picked up the card, ever so carefully, and walked to his bedroom, taking care not to scrunch it each time he leaned his hand into the wall. In the far corner, over the picture of Ryan's mom, he pegged the card onto the makeshift string. He had quite the collection. Just knowing that Ryan had planned it was difficult. He couldn't understand why his son kept trying to reach out. Too many bad things had happened, all at his own hand. He didn't want to mess up another life, or worse, another family.

He lay back on the bed. Somehow, he felt even more alone today. The ceiling fan flapped the cards from wall to wall, a dancing procession of hope. He didn't see it. He closed his eyes and fell asleep.

Blind Trust

12
Blind Trust

*Many Christians come to the place in their relationship with God
where they know that they cannot go deeper with him unless they
surrender everything they are and everything they own. This story is
an analogy of how difficult it can be to make this decision.*

The slave's miniscule boat sat at the top of the
avalanche of water, oscillating slightly from the pull of
the cataract's rush ahead. Peering over the edge of the
boat, the smooth lines of clear liquid powered toward
their destiny.

He knew why he was still there. His master wanted to
reach down and give him a little push, but the master was
waiting for his slave's permission—a strange happening
in natural circumstances. Slaves awaited orders; they
didn't have a choice. This one did.

He knew that the way down would cause him to be
thrown out of the boat. He would be shot in and out
of gushing funnels of strength. Then his meager body
would slap onto the foaming, whirling, swirling eruptions
of water below. The water would punch him, kick him,
spew him from side to side. He might sink to the depths
and never resurface.

He shuddered.

The man was a slave. He had voluntarily sold himself

into the service of his new master. The only thing the master had required of him, before the contract was signed, had been his sin. He had given it gladly. In exchange, he received the master's family name, and he bore it proudly. His back no longer bent over, weighed down by the burdens of his history; he walked tall.

Now the master had informed him of this unusual ritual. Some of the former slaves of the house had escaped the slavery they signed up for to become friends of the master.

"Don't be afraid," they had said. "Once you surrender, there is no turning back, but you will finally be completely free from the cares of the world." This would be his escape, his release.

Yet here he wobbled. Here he wavered.

His old friends kept showing up at the door of his new home. They were mad at him for selling himself into slavery. The voices were all too familiar.

"Come back; leave this new life. You had good times with us. You had control . . . you were free." He could not explain this rite of passage, this choice of blind trust in the master or why it was necessary; there was no way they could comprehend it.

The boat continued to rock gently. His hands gripped the coarse wooden edges all the more as fear played with his mind.

Angels on assignment walked across the water to his side and drew their swords. It was enough to leave his mind free for just a moment. It was long enough.

A surge of courage coursed through his chest. Standing up in his chariot pod, raising his fist, face to the master above, he yelled,

"I CHOOSE FREEDOM!"

His master's hand raced through heaven's walls, through the cloudy sky, through the air to lift up the end of the boat and push him up and over and past the fringes of his past life of slavery toward the eddies that swirled below.

Even before his body hit the torrent, that same hand reached out again. His landing was cushioned. An inner tranquility filled him from the top-most hair of his head to the lowest round curves of his toes. He did not notice, but his garb had changed to that resembling his master's. He was no longer a slave.

A sigh of contentment escaped his lips as he breathed once again. "Freedom," he whispered.

His escape . . . was complete.

Writers Forum: Translation 101

13
Writers Forum: Translation 101

I want to have my writing speak a message to people's hearts.
I want them to be blown away by my depth of knowledge.

My teacher said that I was really good.
I'm actually brilliant, and you'll soon see my amazing talent.

My family and friends have said that they really like my work.
That's proof that I'm as brilliant as I think I am.

I was the best in my English writing class at school.
I'll slam you with my brilliance.

I've sent a query to Doubleday about my first novel.
I'm expecting them to send me a five-digit offer for the rights.

I hope that I can participate in what goes on here.
I am so brilliant that everything you need to know, you can watch and learn from me.

I've written a lot of poetry that I am hoping to publish.
But you'll never see it here; it's so brilliant I'm afraid you might steal it and publish it yourself and make millions.

I feel that God has sent me to you.
So that you can appreciate my brilliance and stoke me with

appropriate kudos.

My writing is so unique, you have seen nothing like it anywhere.
And there's a reason why . . .

I've never taken any kind of writing class or online course, because I feel that I would be taught too many formalities and it would stilt my flair.
I have no idea how to build up a plot to a climax, and I don't even know what syllables are.

My first article is posted, but I haven't had any comments so far. Here is the link.
It's been up there for ten days, and no one has commented on my brilliance yet. Is there no appreciation for talent around here?

Should I really go into the beginner's level?
I'm so much better than that.

Exactly what are the criteria for judging writing on this forum?
My article wasn't placed among the weekly favorites, and it should have been in the top ten, or at least in the top 40.

Wow, those winners had some good stuff!
Maybe I'm not the only brilliant writer.

Exactly how does one go about getting placed?
I'm starting to wonder if perhaps I'm not so brilliant after all.

I've tried out some new things; would you mind commenting?
I'm beginning to admit that the rest of you have some talent too, and I'm using some of your techniques.

Wow; thank you everyone!
Lights going off in brain.

Please red ink me.
I am one of many among my writing peers. I am slowly getting better at my craft, and as long as I stay humble and am willing to learn, I may be really brilliant some day.

Afterthought: Hmm, and maybe I should trash those 3,298 copies of self-published (but unedited) books.

  *The writer vehemently denies any personal experience with abovementioned thoughts.

~

I Can
Smell Him

~

14

I Can Smell Him

I can smell him. His stubble lingers by my cheek. His breathing is quick. Short. My entire body feels as if it is being trailed with a feather. I step back. He nears.

A corner of his lips turns upward. He pulls back so he can see my face. I see the eyes of the man who is my friend. I see the eyes of the man who listens to me. I see one who cares, one who laughs, one who is kind and thoughtful and complimentary. I see the man who wants all of me.

He leans forward until his lips touch my ear. "Tell him you have to meet a client," he whispers. His hand brushes by my waist. I jump. There is that smile again— the one I have been thinking about many times at night.

Only a few hours ago, I lay beside my sleeping husband, and my thoughts of the man I married were utterly benign: *He is so boring. I've never felt truly alive with him. We were so young. We didn't understand what we were getting into. I don't think I love him anymore.* My husband stirred and touched my shoulder. I felt nothing. There was no ache to be close. There was no desire.

Not like now, here. This man moves and my heart stutters. This man . . .

We leave the copy room and return to our desks. He sends me an e-mail. I smile. My insides yearn for him.

My mind is full of opposition. It is as if there is a battle going on. Heavy combat. The scene is thick. The field is full of blood. Swords clash. Shields defray the plunge of the ax. Valiant thoughts lie down and gasp their final breath. The enemy is winning, and the spoils of war are waiting. The plunder is opulent.

I pick up the phone. I hit speed dial to my home. My husband answers.

"Hi, honey. What's up?"

"Oh, nothing in particular. I was thinking of you." I can hear him smile.

"I love you too, sweetie. I need to let you go though; Jake just fell over and needs me. Sorry."

One click, and the line goes dead. Just like that.

The warriors in my mind rouse themselves, watching, waiting. Those they thought dead are resurrected. I rise from my seat and walk down the aisle of office space to my manager's office.

My manager nods his head. He makes a phone call. He scribbles something on paper. "Are you sure about this?"

No, I am not sure, yet I am. There can be no other way.

My heart is being shredded, but I keep driving. The lights spaced five feet apart line the driveway. I park my car. Before my key turns all the way in the door, the door opens, and my husband greets me with a kiss on my forehead.

"What's wrong?" He knows me so well.

"I was transferred to another department. I won't be making as much." Tears fill my eyes.

He pulls me into him. "It's ok. We'll manage."

I wonder if I will ever feel clean again. But at least I can breathe now, and God will give me the strength I need to keep walking away.

The Half-Baked Stranger

15
The Half-Baked Stranger

I've dreamed of moments like these for probably all my life: of children smiling broadly at my feet, reaching out to life and hope; of women weeping softly as they receive all of Christ's love, drinking in forgiveness they never knew existed.

I've dreamed of moments like these: of angels pouring ointment of love and peace and joy over eager masses of fathers and mothers and sons and daughters together.

I've dreamed of moments like these for probably all my life—of standing, watching the Spirit weave his way among this passionate people—such fresh, yet lumpy clay.

But now that I'm here, I cry with joy but also sadness. I can't help but think of all those who I have not reached yet. I have this ball of fire in my hands and mouth and feet, and I carry it forward as fast as I can from village to village, but time is running out for me. . . .

In every village I enter, I wait for a crowd to gather around this half-baked, hunched stranger, then throw out a line and wave the hook in the sea of humanity. I bide my time as my bait of words and stick drawings in the sand burn through the waves of suspicion. PZANG! I catch one. More will follow.

This is my story. This is my life.

I hear my Father calling, just as he called me so long

ago. Then, he told me to go. Now, he is telling me to come.

I don't want to come! I want to stay here. These are my people, the ones I love. But I will come, because he knows best.

So when they take my body and stick me in the ground, they'll want to know what epitaph to etch into the bleak gray stone. My family will say things like, "EVANGELIST RENOWNED," or, "He answered the call," or some such silly rubbish.

I want some substance on that stone. I want to be remembered, not for what I do but for who I am, for what he made me for. I want them to know that I'm perfectly happy to keep on doing up there in prayer what I've been doing down here in person, only I'll have a more supportive group to help me on. (Ever heard of the cloud of witnesses?)

No, nothing fancy on my headstone, please. Just do me a favor and chisel this:

Gone Fishing

Prosperity

16

Prosperity

The couple huddled together on the deck floor of the creaking steamship, eyes straining . . . waiting. A small crowd had gathered with them, all bodies tilting from left to right together with the rise and swell of the tide.

As the fog swirled around their emaciated figures, wisps seemed to curl themselves around Maureen's fingers, up to her very nails that dug deep into Garret's palm every three minutes.

"T'wont be much longer, Maureen," her husband whispered in her ear, encouraging her on. "T'wont be much longer."

Maureen arched her back as her belly tightened up for the hundredth time that morning.

Garrett lifted a finger and stroked it against Maureen's gaunt cheek, his deep love for her obvious to all.

She grinned weakly in return, before another spasm of pain caused her teeth to clench. She lay there amidst heaps of clothes bundled together with rope, a family's precious black kettle leaned up against one such pile. Maureen was grateful for the small provision of privacy the items offered.

Someone had provided a precious sheet to cover Maureen's legs, and a mother of many knelt before her feet, watching for signs of birth.

A man's distant shout rang through the crowd, instantly causing many passengers to move away from the birthing trio. "I see her! I see her crown!"

Garrett jumped up to peer through the hanging sheets of gray fog, and finally he saw her too: the statue recognized by the world as the woman of liberty. Trembling with excitement, he bent down to Maureen's protruding belly. "Hey, babby, we're nearly here!"

As if in response, the baby's foot shifted through her mother's taut, fragile skin and kicked.

Maureen's weak smile was matched by a huge one from the midwife. She poked Garrett in his leg.

"The babby's coming, son. Look!"

Gingerly, Garrett lifted the sheet and watched over the minutes as new life slipped out of its familiar home. Eyes brimming with tears, he waited for the midwife to clear out her mouth before he wrapped the sheet around the warm, wet body and wiped her tiny face. He couldn't remove his eyes from her, and he finally managed to get a few words through his tight throat to his exhausted wife.

"It's a girl, pet. What'll we call her?"

Maureen lifted up her frame on both elbows to see her daughter. Right behind her husband, coming ever closer toward the boat, was the staunch, proud figure of womanhood: a woman who was gripping, yet offering to share the best a mother could want for her child—the torch of light and truth.

"Prosperity," she said quietly, and she reached out her arms for her daughter, put her to her breast, and listened joyfully as Prosperity suckled her first drops of sustenance on the shores of the land of plenty.

That Stalker Thing

17
That Stalker Thing

Sophia lay back on her lumpy dog-haired sofa and thought of Will, a hunk of burning love if ever there was one. Was it his six-foot chiseled body of rippling muscles, or his keen, almost burning mahogany eyes (tinted with gray)? Was it his smile, the way it crinkled at its crooks whenever he looked her way? She sighed a long, lustful exhalation of weakness at the thought of being in his arms. It had to happen soon. She couldn't eat, couldn't sleep, couldn't even think straight.

She'd sent him an e-mail, nothing heavy; she didn't want him to think her a stalker or anything. She'd added him to her MySpace page too. He was listed in her top 8; she had taken great pains to not have him as her #1 friend (stalker thing again).

She wrapped her arms around her body, imagining that they were his. Rubbing them up and down, she wriggled in anticipation of the day when . . . when . . .

All her friends said she was crazy, that Will wasn't interested, that he was out of her league. She, however, knew that they shared something special. Every moment they were together his eyes melted into hers. He didn't see the waistline, the occasional little skin eruption, the small bra size . . . no, Will saw her through eyes of desire too.

It wasn't that they had ever really been "together,"

but they certainly had been in her mind. A friend of a friend of a friend said that Will had a video on YouTube, and she was prone to playing the segment every time she wanted to waft into her reverie. She would turn the lights down low and sway to her favorite song with the butterflies' wing flaps in her stomach joining in.

She journaled about him too:

Dear Journal,

I saw him again today. He was dressed in these baggy jeans that hung on his torso like a god's mantle. You know how I feel, because I tell you so often, but my heart cannot survive like this. I must see him, Journal, I MUST!

Then the day she thought would never happen, happened. She was at the hotel, serving up drinks to overrated customers, when he walked in. She just about fell into the frosted Pina Colada and, without even knowing why, swooned behind the counter.

A deep voice sent her heart a-thumping.

"Ma'am? Ma'am? Are you alright? I saw you fall."

She glanced up, a deep shade of fuchsia, to see his manicured outstretched hand above her permed head. Trembling, she raised her wispy hand out to his, and he pulled her to her feet. His potency surged through her weak frame, and their noses almost touched; his, Romanesque, hers, snubbed.

Up close, she could see that his pupils were dilated. Could it be . . . ? His lips spread out until she could see a hint of his white teeth. She wanted to stretch her mouth forward to press her tongue against those pearly whites, but resisted. This was only their first real rendezvous, after all.

"Thank you," was all she could murmur, and then she set herself to cleaning up the remains of the sticky Pina Colada with an elbow grease ne'er seen before in the Driskell Hotel.

Unfortunately, this is the end of the story. Will Humphries never came back to the bar, but went on to make many other movies starring as the hunk of burning love lover. He never knew what he missed by not returning to the bar that night. Lord knows, Sophia waited long, long after the bar closed in the hope that he would show up. Her visions had fed her for so long that, now that the real thing had appeared, she wanted more. More of Will, obviously, after years of hopeless hope and wasted worship, never meant to be.

Sophia has DVDs of Will's movies in storage, along with the broken shards of coconut-smelling glass (packed in pink tissue paper) and the nylon stockings that she was wearing that night. She has moved on from her employment at the hotel. The memories were too hard to bear. These days, she spends her hours on her dog-haired sofa watching a newer, edgier soap opera that stars a newer, edgier hunk of explosive love. She's only sent him one e-mail so far, posted a vague comment on his blog, and merely has him as her #4 friend on MySpace—that stalker thing again. . . .

~

Scroll and Scribe

~

18
Scroll and Scribe

Timothy's dusty feet appeared first through the old cistern's hole. His sandal fell to the floor with a thump and woke Paul's constant companion, the guard whose wrist was chained to Paul's. Paul struggled to stand, but his sleepy guard tugged back on the chain in protest. Paul's spine fell back against the prison wall. His eyes closed for a moment before he smiled at his visitor.

"Timothy! I am so glad to see you! Do you have news?"

A scroll was placed carefully into Paul's hands in response.

"Bad news I believe. Epaphras gave it to me yesterday— told me that there's trouble in Colosse, and he needs your help and prayers."

Paul rearranged his spine so that it rested in the groove of some rocks. The wax seal lifted noiselessly off the papyrus, and the scroll's form instantly expanded to three times its original size. His gnarled fingers pulled its rolled sides apart, and his eyes began to read. At times he paused, shut his eyes as if pondering the words, and then continued.

Timothy stood on alternate feet to shift the circulation in his legs. The prison, an entry-level room to an old cistern, was damp. The roof was domed, so it was impossible to walk around and hold one's head up, probably a purposeful builder's act.

After what seemed like half an hour, Paul's fingers curled around to carefully re-roll the papyrus. "Wait for a while, Timothy; I must pray."

Time passed. A pot in the corner gave off a persistent fetid stink of the previous day's eliminations. Timothy tried to hold his breath, but when he held it, he invariably had to take a deeper breath back in to make up for the oxygen he had just deprived himself of. The ensuing gag was not worth it.

Paul's back was facing him now. Timothy kicked little mounds of rat poop around the edges of the floor. Some sort of foreign language erupted from the corner and continued for a long time. Feeling sorry for the guard, Timothy began to pray in tongues . . . under his breath.

An hour later found Timothy on the floor, eyes closed as the Spirit ministered peace. A bony finger poked his shoulder.

"Time to write! I know what the Holy Spirit wants."

Timothy looked up into a pair of blazing eyes.

"Timothy, I want them to be blessed. They need to know that our love and prayers go to them all the time, but they desperately need teaching so that they won't go astray again."

Bam! Paul's fist hit the floor, making the guard start. The guard was used to the tongues, but he wasn't used to Paul's outbursts of righteous anger.

"These Gentiles are taking a piece from every religious group traveling through the city and passing it off as their own brand of The Way. They've got Greek speculation, Jewish legalism, and they even have Oriental mysticism! One of the worst parts of this is that they are thinking about worshiping angels: God's servants sent to work with us for the glory of God! All they need is in Christ!" Paul pushed his fingers through what was left of his hair.

"I want them to know that it is all about Jesus. He did everything that was necessary for their salvation. These men are undoing all of the work that Epaphrus put into them, and the flock is listening to strangers rather than their spiritual father. It's reprehensible.

"Jesus, be the center. Be the head, be the crowning glory of this church, and don't let any man take that glory from you." Paul was back on his knees before his Father, dragging the guard with him.

He jumped up again. "I must have the words of the Holy Spirit to counteract the damage done, Timothy, or else it will just be a letter from an old man in prison. The words of the Spirit bring life, and they need new, fresh life in Colosse. CHRIST is their new nature, HE is their holiness, HE is their gateway to the Father. HE has done everything needed to bring them into perfect relationship with the Godhead, and now they are doing things to try to earn that?

"Timothy, write this down!"

Timothy stretched out the fresh papyrus on the driest part of the moldy floor and plunged his reed into the ink.

"This letter is from Paul, chosen by God to be an apostle . . ."*

*Colossians 1:1

The Star of Troy

19
The Star of Troy

Megan was opening the door of her tiny apartment when the mailman puffed up the stairs to give her the parcel. It was an odd shape, and it looked as if someone with less than professional experience had wrapped it. It was big but felt light . . . almost fragile.

Despite her rush to get to the shower and wash away the day's hard work, Megan's curiosity and her penchant for presents got the better of her. After a difficult fight with some blunt scissors, and tape attaching itself to her thumb and all four fingers simultaneously, the brown paper fell away to reveal a Christmas tree star of stunning caliber. She didn't even need to hold it up to the light; it sparkled and twinkled like a winking beau in her hand. That's when the note caught her eye.

Happy Christmas.

Love, Ryan.

Megan sighed the kind of sigh one might imagine an inner-city high school principal making after the fifteenth rebellious youth of the day reached her office. Ryan was her soon-to-be ex-husband, and he would not leave her alone. He was composed of a myriad of problems and shady side jobs even she couldn't wade through. To have to have even one piece of him in her life now was one piece too many, and the glittering star was unceremoniously dumped in the trashcan.

Ryan's star had indeed been winking at her. Ryan's computer had provided an avid inspection of brown paper creases, the sound of thick-edged scissor blades gnawing at tape, a bird's-eye view into Megan's open mouth, and, eventually, darkness, because Ryan's star was really Ryan's private eye.

He hadn't quite planned on it ending this way. He'd assumed that Megan would rush to put it on top of the Christmas tree because of her adoration of pretty things. He'd been wrong. The view from the middle of a trash bag was his reward for the hours of work he had put into his fail-proof spy cam feat. He let his chin drop to his chest and closed his eyes, all hope of finding out if she really hated him gone.

At 7 a.m. the next morning, Ryan's sleep apnea still hadn't finished him off. Over at 201 Freeatlast Apartments, Megan stepped on the trash can foot pedal to throw out her freshly squeezed orange skins. She took another look at the star, which was lying like a hobo on the previous night's TV dinner. She reached in and withdrew the treasure, paused to second-guess herself, and then crowned her Christmas tree with the silver star of Troy.

At 9 a.m., Ryan stretched and groaned in unison with his morning gas. As he blearily groped his way over to his coffee maker, his left eye caught movement on the monitor. Caffeine no longer necessary, his racing heart sat down to watch the Christmas Eve proceedings.

Hours passed. Bernice, his mother-in-law, arrived first, shortly followed by her stoic husband, Bert. Her chatter was, as usual, full of nothing but herself. Bert helped himself generously to the bottle of Johnny Walker he had brought for the party. As his nose slowly turned an interesting shade of red, Martha and Mike showed up with the triplets. Martha got busy while the kids ran amok.

Ryan stared down at Megan's face from his hunting post as she greeted her brother. He'd forgotten how big her smile was.

Mike looked concerned.

"Are you doing okay? I hear that Ryan has been vilifying you no end. Can't he ever point a finger back at himself?"

"You know what they say. What breaks a man makes a man." Megan smiled peacefully at her brother. "You know, Mike, I'm having the best time with God! He's going to get me through this. As for Ryan, I pray every day that his walls of self-protection will crumble and that he will trust God enough to let him into his heart."

Ryan choked.

"Somewhere in that heart of Ryan's is the good part I fell in love with. I hope he lets God help him find it and refine it, for his sake."

Suddenly, Ryan couldn't see anymore. He wasn't sure if it was because of the tears that filled his eyes, or the fact that his hands were desperately wiping them away, but Ryan's private eye had not succeeded in finding out what was going on in Megan's heart; rather, it had exposed, and loosened, a little chunk of his own.

Absolutely Fabulous

20
Absolutely Fabulous

The alarm clock shrilled through the air at 6 a.m. In Patrick's dream, he jumped involuntarily off the thirty-foot cliff in shock.

Is this noise in my dream?

Struggling to regain consciousness before he hit the serrated rocks below, his one eyelid that was not squished into the pillow managed to force itself open wide enough to see what was going on.

Patrick's retina began to send information to his thousands of cerebral neurons that his wife, Dorothy, was getting up! In shock, his pupil enlarged in the darkness to zoom in on the clock. Shifting his body quietly sideways until the other eyelid opened, both waited in tandem to witness the astonishing scenario unfold.

On went the brand new size 16 sweats; back went the hair into the scrunchie. On went the motor of the walking machine; flip flap went the fat on the insides of Dorothy's thighs. Dust flew abundantly in all directions.

True to Patrick's inner predictions, the gasping and wheezing began after approximately one minute, and it wasn't from the inhalation of the dust clouds.

"One tenth of a mile! YES!" She turned the dial and limped to the shower.

Patrick rolled over to warm up her side of the bed,

certain that she would fall back in after her quest for success. His assumptions were proven wrong, but he didn't realize it. He was asleep again, climbing back up the cliff face to Charlie's Angels (clad in black leather) and ready to do some serious damage to the chasing cows that had interrupted his (ahem) spy mission.

"Rise and shine!" Dorothy stood, smiling, behind a breakfast tray of food she had obviously taken quite some time to prepare.

Patrick eyed her suspiciously. She was wearing his favorite cleavage-revealing blouse and had even put on some make-up. Eternity perfume wafted through the air.

"Where did my wife go?"

"Watch it!"

"Oh, there you are." He dared not say another word to spoil whatever it was that was making her act so fabulously charming, and thus restrained himself from asking what the occasion was. He knew it wasn't anyone's birthday, and their anniversary wasn't until the summer . . . sometime . . . so he was safe there.

She sat on the bed beside him, rubbing his arm affectionately. He withheld the idea of a possible rendezvous in the bed later on. Some things were just too dangerous to assume.

"I've had my quiet time; I journaled, worshipped, even did some intercession! Then, I missed your company, so I decided to make you some breakfast." Her suspect gooey beam returned. "I'm off to wake up the kids. You take your time; go back to sleep if you like. I'll take care of everything."

As she softly closed the door, peeking around it once more to send a seductive smile his way, he puzzled over why she hadn't given him the usual "get ready for work" countdown, and then it hit him.

New Year's Day. NO WONDER!

Patrick Dunne swung his legs over the edge of the bed and rubbed his hands together in delighted anticipation. He planned on making the absolute most of the remaining few hours of heaven . . . before his wife gave up on her new resolutions and returned to normal.

Three Days

21

Three Days

His pupils focused in on his son's sleeping eyelids, lit by a trembling candlelight. The eyelashes quivered each time the boy's breath blew up from his loosely closed lips. Even at thirteen, Isaac's face still filled his father with joy, only tonight . . . tonight, a twisting, wringing pain took joy's place.

Abraham tried to reach out and touch the face he adored, but his shaking hand drew back as the tears mushroomed in his eyes. His fingers stroked the hairs of the animal blanket Isaac's foot peeked out from. A guttural sound cracked in his voice, blocking the whisper of love in his throat.

Turning, he caught sight of Sarah at the tent door: face constricted, eyes pleading, fingers and hands intertwining each other frantically, and they both began to weep.

The sun had just begun to awaken from his night of sleep, his forefingers stretching across the sand until they reached into Abraham's tent and flicked away the shadows of darkness.

Sarah was awake, back at the doorway again, her sinking eye shadows betraying the evidence of her sleepless night. She watched him in silence as the minutes passed.

"So." She stopped and took a breath. "So . . . you will obey?"

"Sarah." Their eyes locked; each one seemed to know that the other was trembling, that a skinny spiral of hope still muttered from deep within, that this was not what was asked of them.

"Maybe, maybe . . ." Sarah's face sought out his chest, and the hours of nighttime weeping began anew. Nails bore into his shoulders, deeper yet as he lifted his arms to wrap them about her.

"Father, Mother?" Isaac's sleepy eyes opened wide in consternation as he made his way to their side. Sarah dared not look up. Pushing himself off the floor, Abraham swallowed.

"Son, tell two of the servants to put the saddle on the donkey's colt, and help me chop some wood. The Lord has told me to make a sacrifice in the land of Moriah, and we will be traveling together."

Isaac nodded his head in simplicity of trust and then motioned to Sarah, his eyebrows furrowed.

"But who will stay with Mother?"

Sarah turned her back to the flesh of her flesh and fled.

Abraham tied the last of the wood in place behind Isaac. It would take three days to reach the land of Moriah.

With a desolate sigh, he caught the rope in his hands and began to walk beside his son.

Liberally interpreted from Genesis 22

~

Note Attached

~

22

Note Attached

The chocolate was there in the corner—a cubed box with a purple ribbon tied around its sides. A note was attached. Her smile caught her unawares, swooping past the sadness and tears of the many nights spent alone since it had happened.

She let the swing door slam behind her. Sitting down on the creaky steps of the old porch, she lifted the edge of her hippy skirt onto her knees, pulled out the chocolate orange, and gave it a hefty smack against the boards. Daisy, her Great Dane, now beautifully decorated in purple ribbon, drooled hungrily as Penny savored each swish around her tongue.

She stayed out there until far too many pieces were gone. As she licked her fingers, guiltily, she looked at the unopened envelope. She had just allowed some sweetness back into her life; perhaps she would now allow the gift giver the same graciousness.

The sun pulled the daylight down with it, the silky nuances of dusk wrapping themselves around the strange couple, and Penny's thoughts hovered in their folds. She leaned over to look into Daisy's eyes.

"Should I read it, Daisy girl? Should I let part of him back in this head of mine when I've been trying so hard to keep him out?" Daisy's eyes left her for a moment to gaze disconsolately at the rewrapped chocolate.

"Daisy, this is important!"

The dog's eyes jumped back to Penny's hurting face before they wandered back again to the real point of interest. Sighing, Penny fiddled with her necklace.

Her stomach knocked and rolled as she reached over for the letter. Shifting her body closer to Daisy's, she hesitated before she finally stuck her finger into the side of the flap to begin the staccato cycle of pain all over again.

It was hotel paper.

Dear Penny,

I tried calling you, but hung up before I could pluck up the courage to talk, so now I write. . . .

First of all, I am sorry, so so sorry. I've been the biggest idiot that has ever walked the earth; I know that now. Being away from you has made me realize how much I loved you, and still do.

I know I've hurt you. You probably hate my guts right now . . . and I deserve every ounce of your hate. The more I think about you and what I've done to you, the more I hate myself. I'm such a worthless piece of crud.

Remember, Penny, what the preacher read at our wedding? He read that love isn't all about me? I've acted like it was.

I hope it's not too late. I don't know how you will ever be able to forgive me, but if you do, I will try to be the kind of husband God has always wanted me to be.

Please, Penny, please, will you let me know if it's too late for that? The hotel number is on this letterhead, room number 232. I have to check out by noon, Saturday. I wouldn't blame you at all for not calling, but I'll wait by the phone until then.

Yours,

Slowly, she lifted Josh's letter before Daisy's eyes. "Do you see this, Daisy?" she asked, her tears threatening a major downpour. "He says he's sorry. He wants to come home."

Daisy looked back in deep commiseration before sending a leading glance toward the chocolate again.

Penny shoveled her face into the doggy hair. "Oh, Daisy. What would I do without you? You want sweetness, and so does he, but you are so much easier to love." Her eyes sparked for a moment. She shook her head and stood up.

"Come on, girl; let's get to bed." On their way to the bedroom, Penny stopped by the trashcan to dump Josh's crumpled letter.

Four hours later, shivering in her cotton nightgown, Penny fished it out again. Her feet hopped back to bed over the wood floors and were promptly shoved under Daisy's hefty sleeping body.

"Hey, Daisy," she whispered. Daisy lifted one eyelid slightly. "It hurts, you know?" Daisy's eyelid dropped back into place with an unfeeling grunt, and that's when it hit Penny. With a sigh, she stared at the crumpled ball of an apology in her hand.

She was being offered hope; she could take it at the risk of more pain or remain cynical, self-protective and unforgiving.

Love isn't all about me. Penny picked up her Bible, held it to her chest, and began to pray. . . .

Between Her Teeth

23
Between Her Teeth

I had promised the ladies of our church the best retreat ever, and I was determined to deliver.

My bulletin insert was the most unique ever. I had a friend of mine—that designer, Jean Le Pierre—hand paint a princess with a rose in her teeth onto two hundred pieces of silk. We burnt the edges and then sewed them onto soft leather, with this printed underneath:

She stood upon the balcony,

a rose between her teeth.

She threw him down the rose

and he threw her back her teeth.

The verse represented the theme of the weekend: We are all God's princesses who need to get our teeth into the Word. There was a tear-off paper on the back asking for a rally round of assistance with the work that needed to be done.

Everyone wanted to help. My coup was getting Sylvia Nutmeg to do all of the catering for free. Once she knew she could get away from her six screaming children for three days with a first-rate justification, she was all for it. I must admit, I would have felt the same way. I've met her little darlings . . . from a distance.

We were to meet at the Sledge Hammer Farm for

dinner between six and seven. I made sure it was at least a one-hour drive from the church so that no silly moms would be running home to check on their hapless husbands. Honestly, you'd think they would understand that the world did not fall apart when the men ruled everything.

Once everyone had arrived, we moved on to the meeting room, where I graciously acknowledged my taste in picking Delattia Chia to do the room deco. She had arranged a duo blend of gold and purple chairs and tables, with a chic box (painted on all sides with her own modern art) on each table. She said they represented the six sides of a woman. Personally, I couldn't see how the modern art corresponded to anything, but all of the women oohed and aaahed satisfactorily, and her payment was complete.

Once they had been seated with their non-fat, double-shot, caramel macchiatos, our speaker began. She was so smooth! Every word, every slide shown, every song played swept around the room like leaves whirling in an autumn breeze. A few ladies came up afterward to thank me for such an excellent start to our weekend. Needless to say, I slept well that night, once I had removed the chocolate strawberries from my down pillow.

It was during the next morning's talk that things began to disintegrate. Sadie, one of our lesser-known ladies, arrived in the middle of it, distracting my listening ladies. Worse still, hardly was she seated when she began to cry. I hauled her out of her seat instantaneously, as she was causing a few heads to turn, but when we got to the kitchen, she howled! A few of the table leaders rushed in. Maria gave her one of her buxomly hugs and held her head . . . in there . . . for quite some time. It made me most uncomfortable. Joan, our resident counselor, began to give her some advice on choosing the best times to display emotion. Then Elaine joined in the blubbering as Sadie narrated her tale of woe.

I was counting on the speaker, Angelina Glory, to keep the rest of the group occupied, but the microphone inexplicably went out on her with a pop, along with all of the other electrical equipment we had. She stormed into the kitchen, told me what she thought of my preparation skills, and left! In her wake, she left two hundred women all gossiping in the tiny kitchen about Sadie's personal problems. They were also coming up with possibilities as to what Elaine's problems might be, and questioning if they were in any way similar.

They had just started on their thoughts on how to fix it all when I retreated, and here I am, hiding on my bed under the blanket. It's just Jesus and me in here. He's telling me that I did everything right, I just forgot the most important thing: I never prayed.

It feels as if I've been sleeping on a water mattress for a long time and someone's let the water out. Now my apartment is flooded, and I have to clean up the mess.

Funny thing is, even though it's pitch black in here, I could swear I saw a glint in Jesus's eye when I told him about the electricity going out. . . .

Work With Me

24
Work With Me

Her silver metallic skirt slid up her knees every time she bent a fishnet leg, each one with a nine-inch heeled boot glued on. Delilah was dressed to kill.

She was good at her job. The other girls on de Wallen* knew it, and she knew it. She had to be. Her life depended on it.

She snaked her way around her nightly spot on the stage, a five-foot by five-foot wooden floor fronted by a window. It was there that Delilah sold her product: herself.

Looking out onto the street scrubbed with tourists, Delilah knew he was there to make sure she showed up: her pimp. There Jacobus stayed every night of the week for eight hours, the length of her shift. He made sure that she stayed there to lure customers. He stayed to "keep her safe." He stayed to take half of her wages, and if she didn't get enough business that night, he'd take a little more "for expenses."

She loathed him.

A skinny American stopped and stared at her as she writhed her body parts to imaginary music. He held up his camera. She shook her head. He held up some Euros. Jacobus stepped out of the darkness.

"One hundred and fifty for twenty minutes. She's the best you'll get."

The American dug frantically in his fanny pack for more cash, handing over the last note jubilantly.

"You get twenty minutes, max. Anything other than regular will cost you double. Got it?"

The American nodded his head eagerly, and before waiting for Jacobus's okay, ran for the door into heaven. Jacobus held up one finger to let Delilah know his order, and she obediently followed the American upstairs to her bedroom.

He walked into the bathroom and turned on the shower, making a shhh motion with his finger. "Jetska!" She started for the door in a panic. He grabbed her by her long heel and held on, determined. "Jetska, your dad sent me here."

"Daddy?" Instantly, Delilah's body stopped pulling away. Tears filled her eyes as she pushed her hair back from her cheek. "Daddy?"

"Yes. Your dad hired me to find you. He wanted to be sure that this was the first thing I told you: He says he loves you, no matter what you've done, and he wants you home." Andrew pulled off his sweater to reveal two lightweight harnesses. "Hurry; we haven't got much time. Put this on." He held open one harness for her to step into.

Delilah raised her eyebrows.

"It's for rappelling from the window." He shook it urgently.

She stepped in and let him pull it up her stockinged legs. It tracked through her legs and around her hips like a diaper, as her tears tracked around her nose and cheekbones.

"But . . . my things. . . ."

"No time for that. Sorry." Andrew fastened the buckle on her waist and led her to the window at the back of the room. She stood there, watching him in silence as he hooked a metal wheel to the frame. A large clip clicked onto her harness. He straddled the window frame, beckoning to her to do the same. Time, light, motion; all stopped for her. *Jacobus is waiting downstairs. What if he comes up and finds me like this? What if he beats me . . . ? What if he kills me . . . ?* Her unblinking eyes were shut the moment Andrew slapped her on her shoulder.

"Jetska! Hurry up!" He clipped his own harness to hers and dragged her through the window, her weight throwing both of them into dependence on the clicking wheel and Andrew's rope-release skills to lower them to the ground below. She was still frozen when they hit the ground.

"Jetska! Your pimp will kill you if you keep this up! Work with me, please."

Jetska looked up into his eyes to see what lay behind them, and the life in them startled her. She was so used to death, to darkness, to fear, but here . . . here she felt no fear. He reminded her of how she used to be. Something strong and light and true drew her to her feet and overcame her dread. Adrenaline rushed through her. She threw her hands onto her buckle and unfastened it, throwing it onto the grass with resolve. Andrew's hand was reaching out for hers. Her fingers seized it in determination, and together they began to run.

The de Wallen district is one of the older and better-known areas in Amsterdam's red light district. Prostitutes dance behind windows on the street level to attract their customers, and the girls usually live one floor above their "store." In 2005, 23 percent of the persons registered at the Dutch Foundation Against Trafficking in Women were Dutch citizens.

~

One Blessing

~

25
One Blessing

Her filmy hair caught a whiff of breeze and exposed her eyes. She had been crying. Out there on the swing used to be her favorite place. It still was, but the anguish crowded out the pleasure. Scott was gone. "Gone to meet his Maker," the doctor had said.

His body still lay upstairs. She had lain there by his side for hours, willing him to live again, to come back to her, to his baby. He had not.

Near his body was the crib he had carved, each whittle one move closer to perfection for his baby. He'd always talked about making one, even though the cribs made in China were half the price. She had watched his fingers palpate certain spots of wood to ensure the flow. They seemed to know instinctively what was right, what was not . . . when he was breathing. He had said that he wanted the wood as smooth as her favorite ice cream.

Lisa kicked her feet higher, daring the ropes to just let her go. What was it about a maker who had made a baby but taken the father?

It had only been a few hours, and she already ached for him. She knew he was the one the first time she saw him standing beside the lawnmowers at the gardening store; knew by the gentleness in his eyes; the softness of his tone; the way he listened to her when she talked, even when she had nothing to say. Were he alive at that moment, his full focus would be on her face. His arms would surround her and the baby in her belly, and he would smile that smile of his that let her know she was loved. She wanted to be there now, in his arms, protected, moored to his love. She wanted to watch him treasure her words and feed them back to her in beauty.

He had always said that she would be a wonderful mother. Right at that moment, she didn't want to be a mother. She wanted to be a wife. The swing slowed to a stop. She and her maternity wear crinkled to the grass below, tears and hair entwined with the wretchedness in her chest.

And then, fingers gently pushed under hers, lifting her hand, her arm, her body to a standing position. She stared helplessly at the person in front of her, into the face of a woman who had driven five hours just to be there with her, to hold her and carry her through the throes of loss.

She leaned in to the warm body, tears already weeping onto the welcoming shoulder, mouth open slightly to whisper just one word of blessedness.

"Mom!"

That Carpenter

26

That Carpenter

"It's been two years; two years, and I still haven't found the right face! How can I paint a picture of Jesus when I can't see his face?" Akiane's pucker crinkled up the freckles on her nose.

Her mom twirled one of her eight-year-old's blonde curls. "Let's pray about it."

Akiane's cheeks stretched to accommodate her smile. Grabbing her parents' hands, she looked up to the ceiling and yelled,

"Jesus, we need a model!" She looked back. "I think, we should pray all day this time."

Marcus nodded in silence and grasped her hand a little tighter before he let her go. "Yes, sweetie, let's do that."

That Saturday, angels gathered to grasp uttered prayers as they flew out of the Kramariks' mouths. Love-filled children and adults begged their Father:

"Please, God, send the right man through our front door."

"Lord, we know that you want Akiane to paint a picture of Jesus. Will you find our model and make him want to do it?"

"Lord God, help us to know who you want our daughter to model her picture on."

Racing each other to reach heaven's bowls, the winged

servants filled up one particular container throughout the day until it was full.

"Okay, we've prayed enough now." Akiane got off her knees and went to the fridge door. "I'm starving, Mom."

Meanwhile, angels' hands were carefully tipping a heavenly bowl's contents onto an unsuspecting carpenter. . . .

Dringg. Akiane ran to the door.

"He wants to talk to you, Mom." The smile on Akiane's face suggested that the man was an unusual visitor.

"Ma'am." The tall man nodded respectfully. "You needed some woodwork repairs done?"

She shook her head, frowning. "Why, no. I don't think we called anyone."

"Mom!" Akiane grimaced, her eyes wide in shock at the thought of losing "Jesus." Her body sidled up to her mother's, a hand cupped her ear, and she whispered through gritted teeth, "It's *him!*"

"Oh, oh yes!" She stroked Akiane's hair. "Sir, I'm sorry; we didn't call for a carpenter, but we do have a need. My daughter can explain it to you. Please, would you sit down?" She left the room quickly, certain that Akiane's huge eyes and wide smile would persuade even the hardest heart.

She was right.

Akiane's singing filled the house for the next few days, interspersed with many prayers. "Lord, let me get it right. . . . Jesus, help me to paint you properly. . . . God, fill me with what I need to inspire more people to love you. . . ." She stopped occasionally to bend over her little brother and make him laugh, and it was on one of his chuckles that the phone rang.

"Akiane, it's for you. I think it's that carpenter."

"Hello?" Akiane hooked her hair behind her ear, as if to feel more grown up.

"Hello Akiane."

Akiane's hair covered her face as she walked into the kitchen. Hand on the island, she mumbled through her downed lips. "He says that he's been thinking about this all week, and he's sorry, but he can't represent his Master because he isn't worthy."

"Oh, sweetheart."

Akiane's nose was squished into her mother's prickly sweater. Despite her struggle to breathe, reassurance filled her heart once more. She pushed away from her mom's embrace and laughed. "We just need to pray again!"

A few days later, the phone rang once more.

"Akiane? I tried to argue with God, but I'm sure you know how he is." Akiane and he smiled together. "I'll come over and do this, but I must shave off my beard and cut my hair within three days of doing it. I don't want anyone to . . . I feel as if this is what God wants."

No one would have guessed that the carpenter getting his photo taken on the Kramariks' sofa was going to represent the Creator's son, yet the air was pregnant with expectation. Every angle of his face, his lines, his wrinkles, his hair—all were captured inside the digital box. Long after he left, Akiane sat holding the printouts, tracing a fingertip over his features as if she were painting them already.

Dozens of sketches filled her pages before she felt ready,

but once on the visual boat, her mind drifted easily out to sea.

It took forty hours to fill the huge canvas with the strokes and colors she saw in her mental image, but Akiane eventually finished her masterpiece. It has since brought many to the awareness of the Master's peace, hence its name,

"The Prince of Peace."

"I think God looks at our love. God has everything. He does not need anything except for our love and extended hands." —Akiane. To see Akiane's painting of Jesus, visit this page: http://www. akiane.com/store/

~

Snappy Yellow Crunchies

~

27
Snappy Yellow Crunchies

With her feet on the bottom shelf of the cereal aisle, her longest finger had almost tipped the edge of the box of Snappy Yellow Crunchies when she heard it—the urgent, shocked, offended wail of a child. Susan's arm dropped onto the top shelf, which in turn threw the rest of her torso into disarray until her knees were pressed under the third shelf and her back and arms had flailed into the arms of the passing stranger.

They were strong arms. She tried to mentally slap herself. Men were the last thing on her shopping list, if even!

Susan struggled to find her center of gravity until she had enough of it to pull herself out of her sanctuary.

"Are you ok?" a deep voice asked. When she turned to answer him with her most winsome smile, Susan found herself face to face with a very mannish-looking woman. She must have been at least fifty, and her lower face displayed an obvious five o'clock shadow. With a deep inner sigh, Susan looked the woman in the eye and tried to keep smiling. *Should have known. . . . Darn it! Why do I keep reading those romance novels?*

"Yes. Thank you so much for catching me. It was that screaming child. I was worried."

The woman started to turn back to the Rice Krispies. "Me too. I think she's okay now, though. I don't hear it anymore."

Susan got the message. *Should I leave? Should I say thank you again?* She decided to forget about the Yellow Crunchies. *I've been eating too much sugar anyway.* She moved up to the bran section.

It was while she was calculating the cost per flake of bran that she heard the child scream again. This time, it was practically in her ear. In a 180-degree swing, her eyes landed on what looked like a three-year-old who was struggling to climb out of her cart seat. The harness kept pulling her back, and a very red-faced father was trying to reason with her. *Without the red face, he could look incredibly attractive. Woah! He even has dimples!*

Her fingers clung to the cart handle. *Stop it, Susan. Stop it, stop it, stop it. You are not here to find a man. You are here to shop. Now get on with it! . . . Does he have a ring?*

Susan peeked at his ring finger. There was nothing there, not even a white line.

Nice one, Susan. Now what are you going to do? Think up some lame one-liner? Then what? It'll be like the coffee ad? You find he's living next door and he's run out of coffee and you have six different flavors by the cappuccino machine?

He rolled closer.

"Daddy, Daddy, we need to get dem." A grubby finger pointed at the Flakes of Fibrous Bran in Susan's hand.

A grunt emanated from the child's father, who didn't look Susan's way. *Obviously too embarrassed about the squalling.*

"Daddy!" God's gift to Susan looked down at his child, and, in a moment of tenderness, kissed her curls.

Susan's heart liquefied.

"We have to get dem, Daddy. Mommy said to get

them!"

Susan thrust the box of Flakes of Fibrous Bran into the hand of the surprised father and walked away in disappointment. *I hope they give her mother the runs.*

As she walked out of the store, Susan slapped her cheek, hard. *No more chick flicks. No more romance novels. No more soaps. I do not need a man.* Her weary walk turned into a march. Her hand fished around her pocket for her car keys, but nothing touched her fingers.

An hour later, a van pulled in beside her. The locksmith jumped down from his seat like an agile cat and held out his hand.

"Ms. Levington?"

Susan's eyes wandered all over the locksmith's face. *About twenty-six; very male; fabulous eyes; own business; yum, yum, yum.* She held out her hand, looked him in the eye, flashed her newly whitened teeth, and held on for just one second longer than necessary.

Today was going to be a good day after all.

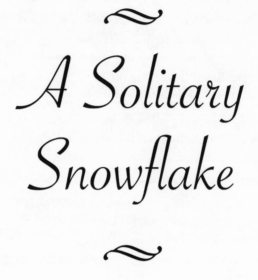

A Solitary Snowflake

28
A Solitary Snowflake

I held up my hand to the snow. A solitary snowflake landed on my mitten. It spread out like the Nile delta: intricate, delicate, superb, special, and then it melted.

The valley filled as the snow fell in silence. It swiftly took over every nook and cranny of life until all the living things disappeared; whiteness and crisp cold air covered them all. My breath curled through the air and floated away into nothingness.

That's when I heard the whimper.

My immediate instinct was to nurture and protect—a long-forgotten feeling. I was the only one left in our bloodline. There were no young ones anymore.

"Hello? Can you hear me?" Silence. I stiffened my chest to quiet my breathing. My heart knocked against its wall.

"Hello? I'd like to help you. Can you say anything?" There it was again, only this time it sounded more like a pleading whine. An animal, perhaps? It came from below the heavy-laden branches of a silver birch. My feet crunched on the frosty carpet as my old body moved to the spot. I tumbled to my knees and tunneled my mittens into the snow.

Hair appeared first, and then a weak tongue reached toward me. He looked like a stray. Panting, I cleared the layers of snow from his body. He did not get up. I knelt there on all fours, half in the hole, half out. The dog's eyes dug into mine. I stopped.

"Charlie! Charlie? Is that you?"

His tail moved.

Hot tears surged under my eyelids. "Charlie! Welcome home!" I let my face drop next to his and kissed his nose repeatedly.

My grown son, Logan, had taken Charlie with him when he left eight years earlier. We'd read about Logan's death on a news site, and I had assumed that Charlie had long since been euthanized at a dog shelter.

Practicality took over. "Stay there, Charlie. Momma's going to get you a treat." I wiped at my eyes with the wet clothing on my hands and looked backward, padding my way out of the snow cone onto more solidified coldness until I could struggle to my feet. "I'll be back as soon as I can; I promise."

His eyes begged me to stay. I shook my head and turned my back on him to face the short walk home.

For some reason, the hospital helper had left my husband's stretcher in the house. We'd used it to move Gareth from his seat to his bed or out onto the porch; we'd even moved him there for his last day on earth, when he wanted to smell the valley he would be laid to rest in. He was gone now, but the stretcher stayed, leaning against the wall in the shed like an old support system.

I tied some rope to one end and pulled it across the snow to Charlie. Gareth would have smiled. I was in mothering mode, determined to see this one survive.

I cracked an egg and reached down with it to Charlie's mouth, which he opened enough to let me drop in the shell's contents. I reached down again with a large syringe of warm milk. His eyes moved with me. The warm liquid was welcomed, a little at a time. Then I dropped one end of the stretcher into the hole and pushed it under Charlie's body. I tried to use it as a lever, but there was too much of him and too little of me.

"Charlie. I need your help." Charlie rolled slightly. It was enough.

With the pole ends pushed into the side of the hollow, I lay on the other side of it and gave his body a push, managing to get Charlie's body onto the stretcher. I rubbed under his ears.

"There you go, Charlie. You ready?"

Charlie's tail moved slightly. I wrapped the rope around my waist and leaned into the snow. The joy that had eluded me would now give me strength.

"Let's go home."

Maud-in-Law

29
Maud-in-Law

Ne'er a minute before he got the box open, she was there, standing over him like the tower of Babel. David's heart sank to his toes. Just two seconds ago, he could have sworn she was asleep by the radio.

"Have you got the instructions, beginning on step 1? Good. Make sure now you have all of the screws you need before you start. Is the screwdriver charged? You know that hand of yours gets bad if you put too much pressure on it. I'll get the other battery, just in case."

Maud's slippers slopped over the tightly glued wood floor to the garage, where she had David's tools arranged on pegs in alphabetical order. Within seconds, to Dave's dismay, she was back at his side. He picked up two of the wooden rectangles marked A and B.

"Careful, Davey boy; those rough edges all need to be on the same side. Remember that time when . . ."

I wish it was time for the hammer so I could drown her out, or maybe even . . . , no, prison for the rest of my life is not exactly appealing, although . . . it would mean a life without Maud . . . then again, it might mean a life with someone in the top bunk called "pretty boy" . . . .

He turned on the screwdriver instead. The buzz produced a suitably rowdy sound.

"No, no David; it isn't time to do that bit yet." Her body was at a 90-degree angle, lips almost stuck on his eardrum,

and she was screaming so loudly his ear was ringing.

Hand on his ear, he put down the screwdriver, glancing fondly at its power. Staring into her face, his only thoughts were of war. Even the mole with the two hairs sticking out of it didn't attract the same attention they usually did.

A staple gun. That would do the trick. A click there right in the middle of that pucker of hers: one to the right, one on the left. Aaaaah, imagine the silence.

Absent-mindedly, he reached down for the first thing that came into his hand. Maud's face screwed up like a kitchen sponge being squeezed out.

Funny, she looks better that way. . . .

"David! Focus on the instructions. Remember that time . . ."

I do remember the time, and the time before that, and the time before that too. How did Nathalie ever talk me into letting her mother live with us? She said Maud would be a big help around the house; that she was one shrewd woman; that she had managed to bring up ten kids on a farm, keep animals, till the land, keep the books, and sell it at a profit. She SAID she would be a great help with the twins on the way, and after.

He shuddered.

Now here I sit putting a crib together with this . . . this woman, and taking it all! This Maud-in-law isn't shrewd at all if she can't read my body language—but knock the 'd' off and you get her in the right class of the species—she's a shrew!

David was powerless.

Lord, God in heaven, help me! If I tell her where to go, I'll never hear the end of it, from either woman. If I throw the screwdriver at her (and it hits her between the eyes in a David and Goliath moment) and tell her to do the job herself, the screaming will wake up the twins in utero.

"David! Are you listening to anything I'm saying? The . . . hammer . . . is . . . over . . . there. Hello? Knock, knock; anybody home?" Maud's gnarly hand was pointing to the floor, the hammer only inches away from her right suede slipper with the three-inch instep.

What would Jesus do, Lord? I did that "finding your purpose" book for eight weeks in church, and her name wasn't in it. I know you have righteous anger in you. Is this a justified time? Can't you just, you know, smite her? What do I DO?

As if from nowhere, a verse came into his mind. He couldn't remember it exactly, but he had learned it as a child.

A harsh word stirs up anger, but a gentle answer stops it.

He knew it was God. A surge of inner strength came into him. He stood to his feet and laid the screwdriver voluntarily on part C of the unfinished crib. He didn't trust himself with it while standing so close to her. David forced a smile through his clenched teeth.

"Maud, I appreciate your help. I know you are a great mother, and that you ran that farm single-handedly for many years, but I'd love to do this alone. These are my first kids, and I want to be able to look at them in their cribs and know that their peaceful sleep is, in part, thanks to me." He picked up the screwdriver again and turned it to "high" before she could get a chance to respond, as every muscle in his body clenched tightly, trying to hold it together.

Please Jesus, please Jesus, do this for me. I don't want to have to go back to anger management class. I gave up twelve weeks of my life for that. I missed so much football! I don't want to walk into church next week with my head down after giving such a great overcoming anger testimony last month. Pleeeeeeease?

"Hrumph!"

Pretty pleeease?

To his incredulous joy and almost divine delight, with a toss of the purple, well-lacquered curls, she left the room, slapping the expensive slippers (that held up her varicose veins) extra hard against the floor to make sure he knew she was not happy. It was unnecessary.

So who is the shrewd one now, Maud? Right back atchya, in your face, the WINNER!

He whirred the screwdriver up to full force and started jumping: a victory dance of manic circles around a few tools and a do-it-yourself kit. The internal self-congratulatory whoops stopped suddenly for an afterthought.

Oh, and thank you, God, for filling me with what I needed to get through this. Amen.

I Have a Gift

30
I Have a Gift

"You have a gift," my mother says. She has said it many times throughout my eighteen years of life.

Women, men, children: I hear their thoughts. I sense their emotions. I see their pain. In my mind, I have invented pictures of every person in our village; so many pictures. Every nuance of voice; every smell of clothes, skin, and hair; every touch of love has meaning. I am not one of the sight-seeing ones as my mother is. I see only darkness, but this gift helps me to see into the soul.

As I sit on the gritty dirt floor of our home, I feel the breeze of my mother's friend rush by my face. Her voice screeches higher than usual with the exhilaration of being the bearer of important news.

Jesus? A movie about Jesus? Who is he? Why do these foreigners want to show us a movie? We are just the Dalits of India—the unwanted in this world, the lesser ones.

Excitement and hope rise to fill the air. My mother squats in front of me and squeezes both my hands in hers.

We wait outside with hundreds, perhaps thousands more, all pushing together like kid goats wanting their mother's milk. It scares me.

The air quivers with silent expectancy. My mother's breathing is rapid. She has never seen a movie before.

An abrupt raucous rattle behind us makes me nervous. I hear hundreds of yards of sari material turn to see.

"It is the box on legs," my mother declares. "Oh!" She turns back. "Light is on the white square ahead." She grasps my hand; the fear of angry spirits and the unexpected transmits to my palm lines as she digs her nails in. The movie has begun.

My mother gives continuous details as the pictures move before the crowd's eyes. I feel their fixation on the screen. She tells me of a baby that is protected from death by the hand of his father, God. She speaks of a river where Jesus stands and argues with the man with wild hair who does not think himself worthy enough to baptize God's son. Then I hear Jesus speak.

"It must be done, because we must do everything that is right."

I feel a shiver go through my body. Something is whirling about this place; the spirits are angry about this movie, yet I sense something far greater and peaceful spiraling about my heart. Do these others sense it too?

My mother tells me of Jesus calling men abruptly from their work, and of their choosing gladly to leave everything for the opportunity to be with him. Her voice rises and falls, her breath slows and quickens, her body joins in sympathy for those she sees.

"Now he is healing people!" I hear her higher voice of surprise muffled by a hand over her mouth. She is astounded by this Jesus.

Jesus's voice shines into my darkness.

"Don't worry about anything. Forgive others. Accept my forgiveness. Trust me."

The words leave his mouth and wrap like the softest sari around my heart. I see into his soul, and I know there is nothing dark in there. *I give you myself, Jesus, son of God. I want to know you. Teach me about you.* A sigh of release escapes my lips. Even though this physical darkness remains, my soul and spirit feel full of light.

Beside this peacefulness, I feel Mother tremble. "Two blind men are following him to his house. They are going into his home!" Her body stiffens, and then I hear Jesus speak to my heart again.

"Do you believe I can make you see?"

"Yes, Lord, we do." Yes Lord, I believe too.

"Because of your faith, it will happen."

I feel a burning heat in my eyes. Salted tears trickle down from the closed lids. My fingers reach up to touch them, but before they make contact, I feel a flutter of soft skin. Light shoots in from all directions at once, and I almost fall over. My mother screams as I grab at her and raise my eyes to hers. The pictures in my mind of my mother's face are instantly replaced. Each line and wrinkle that I have imagined for so long is now part of a truer picture. My lips stretch into a huge smile. As the tears of joy flow further, I whisper,

"Momma, I can see."

I have a gift.

His name

Is

Jesus.

This is based on a true story of a girl in India, blind from birth, who was miraculously healed while watching the JESUS movie:

> » *http://www.jesusfilm.org/*

~

About the Author

~

About the Author

Sally Hanan is an Irish import to the US. She made the perilous eight-hour crossing back in the '90s with a husband and two young children in tow. Since then she has managed to homeschool her above average kids (who are obviously absolute geniuses and extremely good-looking), acquire more "stuff" than she knows what to do with, and house a dog who loves a good belly rub.

On a more professional note, Sally has been counseling people for about twenty years and recently became a certified life coach. She is a facilitator at the Texas School of Supernatural Ministry. She also runs a writing and editing business on the side, because she gets bored easily and she loves fixing words as well as people.

Sally's websites:

> » Coaching & counseling services: Morethanbreathing.com

> » Writing and editing services: Inksnatcher.com

Connect with me online:

> » E-mail: inkmeister@inksnatcher.com

> » Facebook: Inksnatcher

Buy Sally's self-help book on Amazon:

> » *Fix Yourself in Jesus*